Lulu

and the Cat in the Bag

Lulu is a star!

Praise for *Lulu and the Duck in the Park*

2013 ALSC Notable Children's Book

✩✩✩

2013 Book Links *Lasting Connection*

✩✩✩

2013 Booklist *Editors' Choice*

✩✩✩

2013 Chicago Public Library Best of the Best

✩✩✩

2012 Kirkus Reviews *Best Books of the Year*

✩✩✩

2013 USBBY Outstanding International Book List

✩✩✩

2013 CCBC Choice

✩✩✩

2013 ReadKiddoRead Kiddos Finalist

✩✩✩

A Junior Library Guild selection

✩

"McKay shows a rare ability to capture a younger audience in this involving chapter book for transitional readers. The well-structured, third-person narrative builds dramatic tension, provides comic relief of the most believable sort, and shows *plenty of heart*."
—*Booklist* starred review

"A *warmhearted* beginning to a new chapter book series delights from the first few sentences…What Lulu and Mellie do to protect the egg, get through class, and not outrage Mrs. Holiday is told so simply and rhythmically and so true to the girls' perfectly-logical-for-third-graders' thinking, that *it will beguile young readers completely*."—*Kirkus Reviews* starred review

"McKay's pacing is *spot-on*, and the story moves briskly. Lamont's black-and-white illustrations capture the sparkle in Lulu's eyes and the warmth and fuzziness of a newly hatched duckling. The *satisfying* ending will have children awaiting the next installment in what is likely to become a hit series for fans of other plucky characters like Horrible Harry, Stink, and Junie B. Jones."
—*School Library Journal* starred review

....☆..

"'Lulu was famous for animals,' opens this **sparkling** series launch…This offering has…***abundant humor and heart***."—*Publishers Weekly* starred review

....☆..

"McKay introduces complex characters, and animal-loving Lulu's dilemma ***rings true***."—*Horn Book* starred review

....☆..

"Lulu, whose personality reminds me a lot of Ramona Quimby and Clementine, is the kind of good-hearted, bold character kids really relate to and root for." —*Secrets & Sharing Soda*

....☆..

"This is what an early chapter book should be!!" —*LiterariTea*

....☆..

Praise for *Lulu and the Dog from the Sea*

"Whether they live with dogs or not, readers will absorb some truths about family vacations and the true care of animal companions in the company of Lulu and Mellie, who are as ***utterly charming*** and as completely age seven as possible."—*Kirkus Reviews*

........................☆........................

"***McKay hits the nail on the head*** in this beginning chapter book. Children will delight in the story of how this thieving menace turns into a brave hero and loyal friend, wiggling its way into the hearts of the characters and readers alike...This title should be a staple in any early-chapter-book collection."—*School Library Journal* starred review

........................☆........................

"Many kids will sympathize with animal-loving Lulu, and McKay's easygoing, perceptive humor adds liveliness to the account...A lighthearted yet eventful outing, this will entice as a chaptery read-aloud as well as a read-alone."—*Bulletin of the Center for Children's Books*

........................☆........................

Look for more books by

Hilary McKay

Lulu and the Duck in the Park
Lulu and the Dog from the Sea

Lulu
and the Cat in the Bag

Hilary McKay

Illustrated by Priscilla Lamont

Albert Whitman & Company
Chicago, Illinois

Library of Congress Cataloging-in-Publication Data

McKay, Hilary.
Lulu / Hilary McKay ; illustrated by Priscilla Lamont.
pages cm
Summary: "When a mysterious bag is left on Lulu's doorstep,
the last thing her grandmother expects to be in it is a cat—a huge,
neon orange cat. But Lulu knows this cat doesn't mean any harm
and in fact it needs a lovely new home"—Provided by publisher.
ISBN 978-0-8075-4804-2 (hardback)
[1. Cats—Fiction. 2. Grandmothers—Fiction. 3. Cousins—Fiction.] I. Lamont,
Priscilla, illustrator. II. Title.
PZ7.M4786574Lct 2013
[E]—dc23
2013005439

Text copyright © 2011 by Hilary McKay
Illustrations © 2011 by Priscilla Lamont
First published in the UK by Scholastic Children's Books,
an imprint of Scholastic Ltd.
Published in 2013 by Albert Whitman & Company

Printed in China.
10 9 8 7 6 5 4 3 2 1 BP 18 17 16 15 14 13

For more information about Albert Whitman & Company,
visit our web site at www.albertwhitman.com.

Chapter One

The Cat in the Bag

The bag on the doorstep was enormous.

Tied at the top, like a giant shoe bag.

Heavy and lumpy, as if it were
filled with potatoes.

Warm as sunshine, and...

"Snoring!" said Lulu,
bending close to listen.
"It's something alive!"

"Alive?" asked
Lulu's cousin
Mellie,

who was staying at Lulu's house, and she stepped hurriedly backward.

Mellie was a thinker. She could think of lots of alive things that might be in that bag that should not be let out.

"Alive?" repeated Mellie. "Don't just open it then, Lulu! Figure out what it is first!"

But Lulu was already struggling to undo the hard knot of cord that tied the bag. She tugged with her fingers, and when that did not work she tugged with her teeth. She was doing this when she was grabbed from behind by Nan.

Nan was the grandmother of Lulu and Mellie. She was also staying at Lulu's house. She was taking care of the girls while their parents were away. Mellie's mother had won a competition. The prize was a getaway, a week in a hotel in a Spanish city. Lulu's parents had gone as well.

Lulu and Mellie could have gone too, but "*A week in a city?*" Mellie had wailed. A morning at the shops was almost more than Mellie could bear.

Lulu had not been pleased either. "A hotel?" she had asked. "The dogs won't like that!"

"A week in a hotel in a Spanish city is a grown-up holiday!" said Nan. "*I* will look after the girls!"

Lulu and Mellie had sighed with relief.

Nan and Mellie came to stay at Lulu's house so that Lulu's very large collection of animals did not have to be moved anywhere. That was kind

of Nan, because she
really was not an animal
sort of person. Small
creatures, like hamsters,
made her squeal. Larger
ones, like

rabbits, that looked so cuddly
and yet had such sharp claws
and teeth, made her
nervous. Parrots, thought
Nan, were perfect for
jungles—but definitely not
perfect for living rooms.
Dogs were dirty
beasts—large and smelly
and best out of doors.

That was what
Nan thought, but
all the same she
bravely packed her

bag and moved across town to stay with the girls.

"It will be no trouble," she said.

Now, already, on the very first morning, here was trouble. A bagful of trouble, tied up at the top and snoring on the doorstep.

"Leave that bag alone!" said Nan as she grabbed Lulu.

Nan was little and snappy and quick and kind. She was also a good, strong grabber. She hung on to Lulu and she said, "There could be any savage creature in the world in that bag!"

"Oh, Nan!" protested Lulu, while Mellie said fairly, "Not *any*, Nan! Not *any* savage creature! Nothing much bigger than a small crocodile would actually fit. Or a bear cub might, I suppose. Or a bundle of snakes…"

"Mellie!" groaned Lulu. "Stop it! Don't!"

"Don't what?"

"Start Nan off," said Lulu, but it was too late. Nan had already started.

"Snakes!" she cried. "Snakes! Don't you touch it, Lulu! Wait till I get help. Whatever it is, this house needs no more animals! This family needs no more animals! *You* need no more animals, as I have said a thousand times."

"A million times," said Lulu, wriggling away from Nan. "At least. There's a cat in that bag."

"There's more than a cat," said Nan. "One cat is not that size. What are people thinking, leaving such a thing on someone's doorstep? Lulu, come away!"

"Those snores sound like purrs," said Lulu, not coming away.

"Purrs, or growls," said Mellie.

"Growls!" said Nan. "Growls! I'll complain to someone. The police. The wildlife park. The Humane Society. Whoever is responsible for great growling bags on people's doorsteps! I will call them all right now. Lulu—do not touch a thing! Mellie—watch her!"

"Yes, Nan," said Mellie, but Lulu did not say yes too. In fact, the moment Nan was gone she turned back to the bag and began tugging at the knot once again.

"Nan will be mad," said Mellie, watching.

"Poor Nan," said Lulu. "She just doesn't understand about animals. She likes flowers best. There!"

The knot was undone.

The bag was open.

Whatever was inside woke up.

"*MeeeOW!*" said the inside of the bag, and out jumped the most enormous cat that Lulu and Mellie had ever seen.

A glow-in-the-dark orange cat with eyes like lime-green sweets. Fur like a cloud. Paws like beanbags. A tail like a fat feather duster.

"WOW!" said Lulu and Mellie, and they reached out admiring, grabbing hands.

Perhaps the cat thought they wanted to put it back in the bag. It definitely did not want to be grabbed. It leapt away on its beanbag paws, into the street, across fences and gardens. It vanished like an orange rocket fired off into the sky.

At that moment Nan came out again. Neither the police nor the wildlife park nor the Humane Society had been any help at all. They had played her annoying music, and recorded her irate messages on their answering machines, and that was all.

"Useless!" said Nan, who would have liked rescue vans with flashing lights and sirens, and she went back outside feeling grumpy. Then she saw the empty bag on the doorstep, and that made Nan go off like a rocket too.

"Lulu! For goodness' sake!" she exploded. "You opened that bag? You might have been attacked! The minute my back was turned! What a girl! What a granddaughter! Where have you put the creature, anyway? Do you even know what it was?"

"It was a cat," said Lulu when she at last got a chance to reply.

"A cat? There was more than one cat in that bag! That looked like a bag full of cats! Now, Lulu, tell me, where did you put them?"

"It was one cat," said Lulu, "and I didn't put it anywhere. It ran away."

"Like a rocket," added Mellie. "Whoosh, and then gone!"

"Good," said Nan. "Ran away! Good!"

"Bad," said Lulu.

"Listen, Lulu," said Nan, her irritation fizzing away like the last sparks of a firework. "You don't want a cat! You have enough pets, goodness knows. Dogs. Fish. That parrot. Those terrible squeaking things in the shed…"

"Guinea pigs," said Lulu.

"Bad enough having all them," said Nan. "But cats? Worst of all! Bringing in dead birds…Bringing in dead mice…Who would want a cat?"

Charlie, the boy from next door, came along just then, riding his scooter. He heard what Nan said and stopped to look over the fence and say, "We have a cat."

"Yes, Charlie has a cat," agreed Lulu. "A lovely black-and-white one called Suzy. She doesn't bring in dead mice and things, does she, Charlie?"

"Not dead ones," said Charlie cheerfully. "Live ones, though! She's always bringing in live mice. They get under the fridge."

"Your poor mother," exclaimed Nan. "See, Lulu! What did I tell you?"

"Once," said Charlie, enjoying Nan's horror, "you remember, Lulu, because it was at my birthday party and you were there and Mellie was too—there was a bang under the fridge and all the electricity went off. Even my Xbox. And it was ages before it was fixed again."

"Terrible, terrible, terrible," moaned Nan.

"Yes," said Charlie. "I got two new Xbox games for my birthday and I couldn't play either of them. And there was no light or heat or hot water either. Or toast. For days. And all because the wires had been chewed up by one of Suzy's mice…"

Nan shook her head and groaned. Lulu began to wish very much that Charlie would shut up and go away.

"…or maybe one of Suzy's rats," said Charlie.

Nan shrieked, and Mellie got the giggles, the way she sometimes did. Choking, silent giggles, like inside explosions.

"I wonder if anyone's looking for you, Charlie," said Lulu. "Maybe you should go and see."

Charlie paid no attention. He loved making people shriek and giggle.

"Birds are worse than rats and mice," he told Nan. "They can fly, that's why. So they flap around the house smashing things and they go crazy at the windows. You should see the mess the pigeon Suzy brought in yesterday made! Poo everywhere!"

"Charlie!" yelled Lulu. "Do you have to go on and on and on and on?"

"I haven't told you the worst yet," said Charlie. "About the great big…"

Mellie had a very good idea. She picked up the empty cloth bag that had held the cat that was still lying on the step and pulled it over Charlie's head. He stopped speaking mid-sentence, very surprised.

"Mellie!" said Nan. "Take that bag off Charlie's head at once!"

"It's all right, I like it," said Charlie from inside the bag. "Want to see me ride my scooter up the street with this bag on my head?"

"Yes, please!" said Lulu and Mellie.

"NO!" cried Nan, and took the cat bag off his head before he could try.

"OK," he said, looking disappointed. "I better go anyway because guess where my family is going any minute now? (That's what I came out to tell you before you kept wanting to know about Suzy.) Away to the seaside with my friend Henry's family! In two motor homes. My family in one motor home. Henry's family in another motor home. Suzy the cat in her cat carrier. We're almost ready. We've got lots of air freshener and everyone's boots and the metal detector because of what happened last time…"

"Last time," explained Lulu to Mellie and Nan, "Charlie and Henry buried Charlie's mom's bag for buried treasure and the tide came in before they could find where they put it…"

"Was it lost forever?" asked Nan, horrified.

"Yes," said Charlie. "And everyone blamed Henry and me! As if it was our fault that the sea has tides!"

"One of the things that was lost forever was the key to their house!" said Lulu. "We had to help them break in when they got back home."

"We had to break into the motor home too," said Charlie, remembering. "That was even worse because Suzy had been shut in for hours and hours... Gosh! Pooh! It was awful! We had to sleep with all the windows open and Suzy got out and went beach combing and came back with a stinky dead crab. That's why we've packed all the air freshener..."

"Uh!" groaned Nan and went back into the house so that she did not have to listen to any more Suzy stories.

A few minutes later, Charlie (with the bag on his head again) was loaded into a car and driven away. Then Lulu and Mellie were left alone on the doorstep with nothing to show that their mysterious, snoring surprise had ever existed.

"Not even
the bag," said
Mellie sadly.

"Let's go
and look
for it!"
suggested
Lulu.

"Charlie

took it. Didn't you see?"

"Not the bag! The cat!"

But Nan was not pleased with this idea.
"Who in the world would want a cat
after hearing Charlie?" she demanded.
"Anyway, it's not possible to go cat
hunting just now because…because…"

Nan searched her brain for a very good
reason not to go cat hunting.

"Because I am taking you out for
lunch!" she announced at last. "We

will walk through the park and then have pizza and afterward we'll go visiting."

Mellie looked at Lulu to see if she minded doing these things instead of cat hunting. Lulu did not mind at all. She planned to cat hunt all the way to the park and all through the park and after lunch all the time they were visiting friends.

"How lucky I am to have two beautiful granddaughters to take out to lunch!" continued Nan. "Now then, hurry up! Hands, faces, clean teeth, hair, and for goodness' sake, find some tidier clothes!"

"I thought you said we were beautiful," objected Mellie.

"Beautiful? Yes!" said Nan. "Respectable? No! Lulu! What are you doing with that wheelbarrow?"

Lulu explained that she needed the
wheelbarrow to hold the pet carrier.
And that she needed the pet carrier in
case they were lucky enough to find the
runaway cat from the bag. Because if they
did, she would catch that cat and put it
in the pet carrier and load it onto the
wheelbarrow and take it home.

"And that would be perfect!"
said Lulu.

Nan did not think it would be perfect, and she was not very pleased about having to take a wheelbarrow out to lunch. It was rather a nuisance in Pizza Hut.

After lunch, however, Nan agreed that it was a good thing they had brought it along. Then they went visiting a whole collection of Nan's friends. Nan's friends all grew flowers (like Nan did) and detested cats (like Nan did) and thought Lulu and Mellie were wonderful (like Nan did) and gave them strange and useless presents which surprised them so much they kept forgetting to say thank you.

Lulu and Mellie took it in turns to push the wheelbarrow home. Now, as well as the pet carrier, the wheelbarrow held:

A large knitted patchwork blanket.

A rather old teddy bear wearing pirate clothes.

A ship in a bottle that needed gluing.

A very fresh lemon cake on a plate, still hot from the oven and with yellow icing dripping off the top like lava from a volcano.

And an enormous bunch of leftover lilies from the friend with the flower shop.

"Achoo!" sneezed Lulu the moment she saw them, and she continued to sneeze all the way home, and so did Mellie.

"Did you say thank you for those lilies?" demanded Nan.

Mellie and Lulu shook their heads and sneezed four more times each and bumped the wheelbarrow with each sneeze.

"It's nice to say thank you when someone gives you a present," said Nan. "Even for something you might not want...Let me carry those flowers! They are going to slide into the lemon cake any moment!"

Lulu handed the lilies over and Nan began sneezing. She sneezed until she got home, where she thankfully arranged them in a very nice bucket at the end of the garden.

"What are we going to do with the cake?" asked Mellie, lifting it out of the wheelbarrow. It was not as fresh looking as it had been at the beginning of the journey. It was slightly bumped from the ship in the bottle and slightly stabbed from the pirate bear's sword and slightly woolly from the blanket and slightly pollen-dusted from the lilies. It looked more than ever like a volcano.

Nan looked at it thoughtfully.

"Waste not, want not," she said at last. "I'm sure we will enjoy it. Omelettes for supper first. Cake afterward. And by the way, I didn't hear, but I hope you both said thank you!"

They hadn't and they knew it. They had been so astonished at being handed a miniature volcano that they hadn't said anything at all except "Oh!"

"Really!" said Nan. "What terrible manners!"

"I think we *looked* pleased," said Mellie hopefully.

"Let us hope so," said Nan, picking up the cake. "Now, then! One of you come and help me cook supper. The other, unpack this wheelbarrow and put everything away!"

"You go with Nan," Lulu told Mellie, as Nan hurried inside. "I'll put the things away, and then I'm coming out again to look for that cat."

"I almost forgot about it," said Mellie.

"I didn't," said Lulu, who all through the day, at every glimpse of orange (flower or leaf or fur or woolly square in a knitted blanket), had remembered the cat that jumped out of the bag. Where could she begin to hunt for it now, she wondered, as she climbed the stairs with her arms full of presents.

Then she pushed open her bedroom door and found she did not have to hunt at all.

Because there it was.

Wonderful.

Curled up in the middle of her bed.
Snoring.

A gigantic orange heap of fluff.

The cat from the bag!

Beside the cat, a flower, orange, like the cat.

"A marigold," murmured Lulu, who had learned the names of flowers long ago from Nan. "A marigold, and a marigold cat! Perfect!"

Chapter Two

The Cat in the Night

The marigold cat had been asleep when
Lulu came in, but now its eyes were half
open, gazing at Lulu.

"Now what?" they seemed to ask. "It
has been a bad day. Thrown out of my
home. The time in that bag. No food.
No peace. Nowhere to rest (until I found
your window open). Now what?"

Lulu understood. She had always found
it easy to think the way an animal does.
She could guess that although the cat

on her bed looked as soft and relaxed as a cuddly toy, underneath its fluff it was wondering: *Do I need to jump out the window? Or not?*

That was why she did not rush to stroke or cuddle the marigold cat. Instead, she tried to make it feel as if lying on her bed was a safe and normal thing to do.

"Don't worry," she murmured to the cat as she began arranging the presents. "Don't jump. Don't worry about me at all."

Mellie had brought a chair to sleep on that unfolded at night into a little bed.

The cat watched as Lulu spread the patchwork quilt over it.

It yawned when she sat the pirate bear on the windowsill.

It blinked while she uncorked the ship in the bottle and peered thoughtfully inside.

When Nan called "Supper!" Lulu left everything where it was, the blanket on the chair, the bear on the windowsill, the ship in the bottle, and the marigold cat curled on the bed.

I don't need to jump out of the window, thought the cat thankfully.

There was always a lot to do at the end of a day in Lulu's house. The ancient parrot liked to be scratched and talked to while he watched his favorite cooking show. The guinea pigs needed fresh hay and carrots. The old dog, Sam, had to be given his old dog medicine. The young dog, Rocko, had to be worn out with wild chases up and down the little garden. Last of all the rabbits had to be taken from their runs and put to bed. The boy rabbits in the boy rabbit hutch. The girl rabbits in the girl rabbit hutch.

Nan and Mellie helped with all these jobs. Nan measured out medicine and Mellie threw balls for Rocko. Nan found the right TV channel for the parrot. Mellie washed the guinea pigs' carrots. Nan was very strict with the rabbits.

Lulu did the rabbit catching, the hay cleaning, the poo removing, and the parrot scratching. All the time that everyone was working, Nan talked about how many pets Lulu had compared to the number Nan thought it would be sensible to have.

"Guinea pigs!" she said to Lulu. "Now, Lulu, that is very interesting. Guinea pigs are not meant to be pets at all...No! In South America, did you know they are eaten as food? That's what guinea pigs are *meant* for! Not keeping as pets in a shed!"

"Nan!" exclaimed Mellie. "Would you really like to eat Socks and Mittens?"

Nan said of course not. What a suggestion! Terrible! She was only explaining why guinea pigs were such very bad pets. And also she wondered if Lulu had ever thought that it might be a good idea to give both the guinea pigs and the rabbits to the pet farm in town, where Lulu could visit them whenever she liked.

"And then there would be none of this cleaning out," explained Nan. "Or sawdust or smells or worrying every night if all the rabbits are where they should be..."

"You don't have to worry," said Lulu. "One little mix-up wouldn't really matter."

"Oh yes it would, Lulu!" said Nan. "Oh yes it would! And another thing! About the dogs..."

The dogs, who had been listening, now pricked up their ears. They always knew when they were being talked about. They also knew how much they bothered Nan. They always had. Every time one of them ate a letter or licked out a bowl on the table or sat down suddenly just where she was walking or fell asleep in a doorway or rolled muddily on the sofa, she got angry. The fuss she made when they did their mad barking at the visitors was awful. *Nan*, thought the dogs, *fussed about everything.* Play-fighting in the kitchen. Eating soap in the bathroom. Bones in the living room. She thought they were bad dogs.

"The pet farm doesn't have dogs," remarked Lulu cheerfully. Nan's plans to get rid of her animals did not worry her at all. Lulu was used to them. Nan thought of new ones every time she visited.

"Very sensible of the pet farm," said Nan. "But listen, Lulu! I have a very kind friend who would be glad to have an old dog like Sam for company."

"But would they like Rocko too?" asked Lulu wickedly.

"It would be unkind to split them up," agreed Mellie.

"Rocko, no," admitted Nan, looking in disgust at Rocko, who was chomping a mouthful of guinea-pig food, swallowing the bits he liked, and letting the rest dribble all green and slimy from the corners of his mouth.

"I can't think of anyone who would be glad to have Rocko," admitted Nan. "Not as he is! But I am sure there are dog training classes that he could go to. I have seen them on television, absolutely dreadful dogs, nearly as bad as him, taught to sit and walk…"

At the word "walk," Rocko flung himself with delight at Nan and tried to kiss her with green slime kisses. Lulu grabbed him just in time, while Mellie began her exploding giggles again.

"Lulu," ordered Nan, "before you do anything else, please wash that dog's face!"

Lulu washed Rocko's face with goldfish water.

"You haven't thought of a way of getting rid of the goldfish yet," Mellie reminded Nan.

"The fish are easy," said Nan. "The pond in the park is full of fish. A few more would do no harm."

"And the parrot?"

"I'm sure he could go to the pet farm with the rabbits," said Nan. "It would be

a nice change for him. All he does is sit on top of that cage all day."

"He likes sitting on top of his cage," pointed out Lulu. "He could sit anywhere else if he wanted. He doesn't like change. He's very old."

"How old?"

"More than eighty," said Lulu.

"Good gracious heavens!" cried Nan. "Then he should be in a museum! At least let us thank goodness that bag full of cats disappeared. Cats are the worst!"

"What, worse than Rocko?" asked Mellie, and her giggles, which had never really left her all afternoon, began again.

"You heard what Charlie said about the cat they have next door! How sorry I am for that boy's mother!"

"Lots of people are sorry for Charlie's mother," remarked Lulu. "But not because of his cat!"

"Well, well," said Nan. "Charlie is in his motor home and the animals are put away for the night! We can forget them for a while. Come along now! It's been a long, long day. Who'll fetch my bag from my room?"

Mellie was the closest to the stairs, and she was halfway up before Lulu could begin to rush after her.

"Not in your *shoes*, Lulu!" exclaimed Nan, stopping her as she passed. "And I didn't see you wash your hands either! Back into the kitchen, please!"

Lulu kicked off her shoes, scrubbed her hands at the kitchen sink, and waited in agony for Mellie to appear and announce, "You'll never guess what I just found upstairs!"

It didn't happen.
Mellie seemed to
be gone for a very
long time, but she
returned with the
bag and handed it

to Nan without a word about marigold
cats. Lulu looked at her anxiously.
Had she seen or hadn't she? Perhaps
she had just gone into Nan's room.
Perhaps the cat had changed its mind
and jumped out of the window after
all. Perhaps...

"That patchwork blanket looks very
nice on my chair," said Mellie sweetly,
ignoring Lulu's glares.

"I hope you said thank you for it,"
remarked Nan a little vaguely. "Come
with me now, Lulu, and see what I
am making."

Nan did not knit as many grandmothers do. She made things with beads strung on thin silver threads. She got out her beads and wires from her bag and showed Lulu the necklace she was making, a rainbow loop of flowers. "Almost finished," she said. "Then I will have two. One for you…" Nan yawned a tiny, ladylike yawn "…one for Mellie. Hmmm, hmmm," said Nan sleepily and closed her eyes.

Lulu, who had been holding the flowery necklace to admire it, laid it very, very gently on Nan's knee.

Nan did not move.

Silently, Lulu stood up.

Across the room and just as silently, Mellie did the same.

Nan gave a very small snore.

Lulu's eyes met Mellie's. Mellie, Lulu could see, was about to explode. Nan snored again, and Lulu shot across the room, grabbed Mellie, and dragged her to the kitchen.

"Oh! Oh! Oh!" gasped Mellie, bent over and shaking. "Two snores! Lulu, that cat's asleep on your bed, did you know?"

Lulu nodded.

"What'll we do?"

"Feed it," said Lulu. "Quickly, before Nan wakes up. Oh, Mellie, please don't snort! Help me instead!"

She began to load a tray. Tuna fish. Water. Milk. Cheese crackers. Cold ham. Mellie recovered in time to add a leftover omelette. They carried it upstairs and pushed open the bedroom door. The marigold cat looked up worriedly, measuring the distance between itself and the window. "Look!" whispered Lulu and lowered the tray,

and the cat looked and began to purr
like an engine.

Just as the marigold cat was the largest
cat by far that Lulu and Mellie had ever
seen, so the marigold cat's purring was
the loudest they had ever heard. It purred
as they stroked it. It purred as it chewed
up everything on the tray. It purred even
when wrapped in the patchwork quilt.
It purred by itself alone in the bedroom
when they took away the supper tray and
crept back downstairs to wash the empty

plates. They could hear it in the kitchen, and they could hear it in the living room, and in her dreams, Nan heard it too.

"Was I snoring?" she asked, waking up with a jump. "Lulu, I dreamed I heard myself snoring! It can't be true! I never have! Snoring! Was I? Now, Mellie, tell me the truth!"

Mellie became speechless with giggles and had to lie on the floor.

"Lulu?" asked Nan pleadingly.

"You were snoring a little tiny bit, but hardly anything at all," Lulu told her truthfully.

Nan looked as horrified as if Lulu had said, "Your head was falling off a little tiny bit, but hardly anything at all."

So Lulu added kindly, "But I don't think that's what you heard…"

Lulu paused. There was no sound from upstairs anymore. No purring. Nothing.

And anyway, what could she say? "I think you heard the marigold cat?" Of course not!

"Perhaps a helicopter flew over," she suggested to Nan. "Maybe you heard that. Or a motorcycle, revving up. A lawn mower, even…"

"Helicopters!" wailed poor Nan, who up until the last few minutes had believed she spent all her sleep hours in ladylike silence. "Motorcycles! Lawn mowers! I sounded like that! Tomorrow I will go to the doctor!"

"For snoring?" asked Mellie, rolling around on the carpet, and she laughed so much that Lulu could not help joining in too.

Suddenly, in the middle of the laughter and in the middle of Nan's wailing, came a sound that startled them all into silence.

Heavy feet. Beanbag feet. Treading hard and loud, creaking the floorboards of the room overhead.

Sam and Rocko, who had been dozing by the fire, woke and put back their ears and growled. All down the middle of their backs a line of fur stood up like grass.

"What is that?" whispered Nan.

Lulu and Mellie knew what it was of course: the marigold cat. What else could it be?

"A ghost?" asked Lulu hopefully.

The dogs began to bark.

Nan was on her feet. She did not believe in ghosts. She believed in burglars. She was not afraid of them, though. She was not afraid of anything (except being heard to snore). Brave as a lion, she rolled her magazine into a weapon, ordered, "Girls—stay here with the dogs!

Dogs—guard the girls!" and charged up the stairs.

Lulu and Mellie charged after her.

The dogs did not. They dared not. They knew who was the boss. Nan. "Dogs Downstairs" was the absolute rule when Nan was visiting. Not even the smell of the most enormous marigold cat in the world could entice them to break it. They stayed at the foot of the stairs whimpering and yowling while Lulu, Mellie, and Nan hunted through the two bedrooms and the bathroom and the linen closet.

And found nothing but flowers. Two flowers. A marigold on Lulu's bed. A blue flower like a star, caught on the windowsill.

"Love-in-a-mist," said Nan, closing the window. "Lulu? Mellie?"

"Mmm?" they said.

"Is there something you're not telling me?"

Lulu and Mellie nodded.

"Something bad?"

"No, no! Very nice."

"About these flowers?"

"Yes, very nice about the flowers," agreed Lulu, and all at once began yawning and yawning. Mellie caught Lulu's yawns, just as Lulu had caught Mellie's giggles, and suddenly they could not stop.

"Bed," said Nan. "And sleep. And sweet dreams. No ghosts! What a silly idea!"

"Yes," agreed Lulu.

"Burglars are impossible. With two dogs downstairs…" She glared down the stairs at the dogs, who rolled on their backs to show they understood.

"…and me upstairs in the room next door. What could be safer?"

"Nothing," said Lulu and Mellie, hugging her.

They went to bed with their windows closed and their bedroom doors open so that Nan could rush to the rescue at the slightest sound. With her magazine.

"Not that I will need to," said Nan.

The house became dark. And quiet (except for the gentle sound of helicopter snoring). Mellie on her chair bed snuffled with giggles in her sleep. The dogs ran in dreams with silent, twitching feet. Only Lulu was awake.

Very quietly, Lulu crept out of bed and opened her bedroom window again. And soon afterward the beanbag paws began creaking the floorboards, just like before.

"Lovely, lovely marigold cat," murmured Lulu, more asleep than awake, and then completely asleep.

After that neither Lulu nor Nan nor Mellie heard a single sound all night.

Daisies, catmint, and feathery grasses. Poppies. More marigolds. More love-in-a-mist. Flowers on the landing. Flowers on Nan's bedside rug. Flowers on the bath mat.

But most of all on Lulu's bed, where the marigold cat, tired out with all its hunting and collecting, curled up into a huge, orange, snoring, purring heap of fur.

And was discovered by Nan in the morning.

Chapter Three

The Cat and the Dogs

"Well!" said Nan indignantly, gazing at her sleeping granddaughters and the sleeping, snoring marigold cat. "Well!"

And she went and fetched her magazine and rolled it up again.

She used it to prod, very gently, the marigold cat.

The marigold cat gave one last snore and opened its eyes and blinked at Nan. It smiled a curly, cat-shaped smile. It seemed to understand that Nan was no danger. Then it stretched and jumped from Lulu's bed and landed with a thump and a burglarish creak of floorboards beside Nan.

Lulu woke first.

Very slowly.

Pushing her face in her pillow.

Yawning.

Remembering.

Stretching out a hand for the marigold cat.

"Are you still there?" she asked sleepily. "What were you doing all night, in and out of the window? Are those more flowers? Oh!"

"Yes, oh!" said Nan sternly.

"Hello, Nan!"

"Hello, Lulu."

"Look at all the flowers."

"I am looking at the flowers," said Nan. "And at the other thing. This orange,

snoring thing! (Didn't I tell you, Lulu, that I never snored!) This jumped-out-the-bag-and-ran-away thing! Run away again!" Nan told the marigold cat.

The marigold cat hooked up a stem of love-in-the-mist with its beanbag paw and laid it at Nan's feet like a present.

"It likes you," said Lulu, and Mellie

rolled over and said sleepily, "Course it does."

The marigold cat stayed for breakfast. Scrambled eggs. Dog biscuits, cereal and milk, all served by Nan.

"I have never starved anyone yet," said Nan. "And I am not about to begin now. But, Lulu, you cannot keep that animal! Just listen to those dogs!"

The dogs had to be shut outside while the marigold cat ate breakfast. They were outraged. The old dog Sam squashed his nose into the crack under the door and bayed. The young dog Rocko leapt up and down outside the kitchen window. Every time he popped up he woofed one very loud, shocked woof. Every time he vanished he growled.

The noise was so much that nobody heard the postman knocking outside. So he pushed the door open instead and began to announce, "Your dogs are going crazy out here," but the last two words were said from flat on the floor, as he was knocked down by Sam and Rocko, charging in to confront the marigold cat. They ran in a straight line. Over the postman. Over chairs. Barging under the table, shaking off the plates. Mellie shouted. Lulu dived to grab their collars. Nan waved her magazine over her head. The marigold cat swelled to an enormous size.

Biff! went a beanbag paw. Once on Rocko's nose. Once on Sam's.

"WOW!" yowled the dogs, and turned and ran, back the way they had come, knocking down more chairs, more plates, and Mellie as they passed. The postman was trampled again. Nan and the marigold cat remained standing.

After that the dogs were miserable. They lay on the grass and held their noses and cried. Even when Lulu lured them in with biscuits they were not happy. They crawled past the marigold cat, shivering. The marigold cat sat on the bottom stair and washed her biffing paw thoughtfully when they passed.

The dogs stopped wanting to go upstairs. They stopped trying to lick

plates on the table. They stopped falling
asleep in inconvenient places. They got
in their baskets without being told. In
their baskets they yowled and growled
nonstop. Nothing anyone could do would
comfort them.

"Nan's right," said Mellie. "The
marigold cat can't stay here. It's not fair
to the poor dogs."

Lulu knew that was true. The dogs had
no peace, and neither did the marigold
cat. It was trying to make a flower

collection, but wherever it went with its flowers, there was a fuss.

In the living room was the parrot. He sat safe out of biffing range on top of his cage and shrieked and flapped at the poor marigold cat.

It was not peaceful in the kitchen either with the dogs in their baskets,

yowling and growling and holding their noses. And where the dogs did not go, Nan went.

"Not in there please, your majesty!" she said when the marigold cat, looking for a

little quiet,
curled up in
a marigold
heap in the
linen closet.

"Out you
come!" she
ordered when
the marigold cat began a daisy collection
under Lulu's bed.

Nan divided the marigold cat's flower
collection between the vases and the
compost heap, depending on how healthy
the flowers looked.

"What kind of cat are you?" she said to
the cat. "Terrifying the dogs! Scaring the
bird! Gathering flowers! What kind of a
cat is that? If you *are* a cat!"

It was Mellie who noticed that when
they went shopping Nan bought a packet

of salmon-flavored cat treats and hid them in her bag.

"Nan," said Lulu hopefully, "the dogs don't like the marigold cat. But I think you do."

"Is that what you think?" asked Nan.

"Yes, I do," said Lulu, "and so does Mellie. And we have been wondering if when you go home the marigold cat could go too, to live with you."

"Is that what you've been wondering?"

"Yes," said Lulu.

"Yes," said Mellie.

"Just because you like something doesn't mean you want it to come and live with you," protested Nan. "For instance, I like your friend Charlie, but I wouldn't want him to come and live with me…"

"Charlie is different," said Lulu.

"He's bonkers," said Mellie.

"It's not fair to compare the marigold cat to Charlie," said Lulu. "They're not at all alike."

The marigold cat, who had been listening to the conversation, blinked in agreement.

"Well then, not Charlie," said Nan. "Someone else! The Queen of England! I like her too, but I also wouldn't want her to come and live with me. (Although I wouldn't mind a short visit.)"

"How short?" interrupted Mellie.

"Three or four days. But as for that enormous marigold cat, it is just not my problem! *You* should not have let it out of the bag."

"Nan!" said Lulu reproachfully.

"I am not a cat person. I am a garden person."

"The marigold cat is a garden cat," said Mellie, and as if to prove it, the marigold cat went out and found a new flower for Nan from the front garden.

"Hmmm," said Nan. "Chickweed. Flowers from the garden of every house on the street. Weeds from here."

"We tried planting flowers," said Lulu. "But the dogs dug them up as fast as we planted them. They're no good at gardening. They don't understand. But I'm sure the marigold cat would be different."

"I'm sure the marigold cat would be the same," said Nan.

Lulu did not argue anymore. She went to the shed and fetched a garden spade. Mellie went with her and collected a garden fork.

"What about those silly dogs?" asked Nan.

The marigold cat sat down by the flower bed and cleaned its biffing paw.

That day, in between zookeeping and dog walking and cat food shopping, Lulu and Mellie dug the flower bed.

The next morning they went with Nan to the market for plants. In the middle of the flower bed they planted a little green bush. All around the edge, a circle of pansies—bright colors like the beads Nan wove into necklaces.

Rocko and Sam could hardly stand it. They longed to garden as well. They longed to scoop out dog-shaped hollows and roll in the dust. They longed to dig for interesting bones. They longed to scrabble large holes, like rabbit traps. They longed to scratch up the pansies and gnaw the roots of the little green bush. That was the dogs' sort of gardening.

It was not the cat's sort of gardening, and it would not allow it.

It sat on guard under the little green bush, and when any dogs came by it got its biffing paw ready. It biffed Sam when he arrived with his smelly old bone, looking for somewhere to plant a smelly-old-bone tree. When Rocko sneaked past  and grabbed a pansy, the marigold cat chased him all across the yard.

"Perhaps you are a garden cat," said Nan, getting out her cat treats.

The dogs gave up trying to garden and went to sulk in their baskets instead. They glared at the marigold

cat from between
their paws, as
if they were
thinking of
vanishing
magic.

Perhaps they
were thinking of vanishing magic.

The very day after the flower bed was
planted, the marigold cat disappeared.

Chapter Four

The Cat and the Flowers

One day the marigold cat was there, eating enormous meals three times a day, organizing the dogs, bringing in flowers, curling up in dark places from which it was chased.

The next it was gone.

It was nowhere in the house. The dogs proved that. They came joyfully out of their baskets and began making up for lost time, grabbing things off the table, sleeping in doorways, chewing

up the mail as it came through the
mailbox.

Nan called the police. The Humane
Society. The wildlife park people. All
her friends. Everyone she could think of
who might know how to find a cat.

No one was any use.

Then Lulu and Mellie and Nan were
very sad. They imagined all the terrible
things that might have happened to the
marigold cat.

Starving.

Run over.

Kidnapped.

Back in a bag (poor thing).

To cheer them up, Nan's friends came
to visit to say how sorry they were to
hear that the wonderful animal, about
whom Nan had told them so many good
things, had suddenly vanished. They were

all very kind and they all brought presents
for Lulu and Mellie. The presents (half
a bottle of lavender perfume, a woolly
hat, a CD of Christmas carols played
on a trumpet, and a book about jungles
without any pictures) were so surprising
that Lulu and Mellie had to be reminded
to say thank you almost every time.
Instead of what they usually said, which
was, "What! Is that for me? Oh my!"

"It is good manners," Nan reminded
them, "to say thank you when someone
gives you a present."

"Yes, Nan," said Lulu and Mellie.

Each time one of Nan's friends
visited, Nan told the story of the
marigold cat again. How she had at
last found a perfect pet. A flower-loving,
dog-controlling, perfect pet. Each time
the story got a little bit sadder.

The dogs were not sorry the marigold cat was gone. They were very glad. You could tell by the way they swaggered through the house, their eyes gleaming, their tails like flags of victory.

"You don't need to be so pleased," said Lulu huffily "Because I am going to find that marigold cat! And you," she added, suddenly inspired, "are going to help!"

The dogs nearly fell over laughing with their tongues hanging out.

"Never, never, never!" they seemed to say.

"Oh yes, you are," said Lulu and clipped on their leashes.

"How, Lulu?" demanded Mellie. "How could they possibly help?"

"The police use dogs for tracking," said Nan, looking almost a little hopeful.

"*Brainy* dogs, though," said Mellie, and Nan stopped looking hopeful. Rocko's leash was already tangled around his unbrainy legs. Sam had forgotten he was wearing one and was trying to walk under the fence.

"They're not very brainy," admitted Lulu, untangling Rocko and hauling back Sam, "but I think they might be brainy enough."

They started in the yard. They had searched it before, but not with the dogs. Lulu watched them closely as she led them around. By the edge of the fence. In and out of the guinea pig shed. Nowhere near the garden. (The dogs no longer cared for gardening. The biffing monster had seen to that.) All along the rabbit hutches, though, and under the bushes.

The dogs remained as cheerful
as ever.

"They wouldn't look like that if the
marigold cat was hiding in the yard,"
said Lulu. "We'd better try the street."

Nan waited at the gate while she and
Mellie set off together.

"Down to the end one way," said
Lulu, "and then back and past the gate
and down to the other end. And then
we'll cross over. Come on!"

It was a sunny, friendly evening. Lots of neighbors were out in their gardens. "Do you mind," asked Lulu and Mellie, "if we come and look for a cat?"

No one minded, and so Lulu and Mellie and the happy-tailed dogs looked at gardens with poppies, love-in-a-mist, and daisies. Gardens with roses and long tickling grasses. Gardens with weeds and gardens with vegetables.

They went all the way to the end of the street and back to Nan at the gate without a hint of the marigold cat.

"Now we'll try the other way," said Lulu.

The dogs looked less cheerful. Rocko had been hoping that now they would go to the park. Sam thought it was high time they went home and did some more annoying of Nan.

"The other way," insisted Lulu, tugging their leads.

The other way was not so interesting. They raced past Charlie's house and the one next door to it that was as neat as a painted picture. They went right to the corner where Henry lived. "That's far enough!" called Nan from the gate, so they turned again, the dogs now very bouncy because their noses were pointing toward home, Lulu and Mellie walking slowly, inspecting the flowers in every garden.

"Marigolds in Charlie's," said Lulu. "I didn't notice before."

They paused to look. Charlie's house seemed half asleep with no family home and no Suzy on the windowsill.

The dogs did not want to stop at Charlie's house. They tried to pull Lulu and Mellie past. Their eyes were no longer gleams of mischief. Their tails no longer waved like flags.

"Aha!" said Lulu and opened the garden gate.

The dogs sat down and looked mutinous.

"Let's go around the back," said Lulu. "No one would mind. They'd know we're not burglars. Come on, Mellie! Come on, dogs!"

Very, very grumpily the dogs slouched after Lulu and Mellie.

Along the little path.

Around past the picnic table.

Into the back garden.

It was extremely quiet.

No Charlie. No Charlie's family. No Suzy. No birds on the empty bird feeder. No sign of life...

Except...

One wilted marigold caught in the cat flap.

Down on her stomach went Lulu, peering through the cat flap.

The dogs moaned in despair, and they pulled on their leashes to pull Lulu away.

But Lulu saw.

The marigold cat had found a peaceful place for its flower collection at last. A trail of flowers led across the kitchen floor. There was a whole heap in the corner by Charlie's rain boots. And on top of the heap, like an indoor bonfire, curled up and snoring (or maybe purring) slept the marigold cat.

"Nan! Nan! Nan!" screamed Mellie, dashing back into the street with the dogs behind her. "We found it! We found it, on a heap of flowers in Charlie's kitchen! Lulu's there now, watching through the cat flap!"

"Good gracious heavens!" cried Nan. "What a wonderful thing!"

"Come and help us break down the door!"

But it was not necessary to break down the door. Because ever since Charlie had buried his mother's bag for buried treasure and the family had returned from vacation to find themselves locked out, a spare key had been left at Lulu's house just in case. And while Lulu watched through the cat flap and Rocko and Sam moaned in despair, Mellie and Nan hunted out that key and opened the door.

And then they stared and stared and stared and stared.

And the marigold cat opened her eyes and purred and purred and purred and purred.

"I have to sit down," said Nan, and she did, at Charlie's mom's kitchen table, with her head in her hands.

The marigold cat looked at Nan from among its orange cloud of fur, blinking its lime-green eyes, swishing its feather-duster tail. Then, very slowly, on beanbag paws, it padded across to Nan.

The marigold cat was carrying something yellow, which she laid at Nan's feet.

A marigold kitten.

And while Nan was saying, "Oh! What! Oh! Oh my goodness!" the cat fetched another.

Two marigold kittens.

Nan swallowed and mopped her eyes and her mouth opened and closed, but she did not say a word.

"Nan," said Lulu, while Mellie exploded in a heap of giggles, "if someone gives you a present, it's nice to say thank you!"

When Nan went back to her own house the cats went too, and the first thing she did when she got there was invite all her friends to admire them.

At Lulu's house, Rocko and Sam
crawled out of their baskets and sighed
with relief.

"We named them Dandelion and Daisy," Lulu told Charlie when he returned from vacation. "Dandy and Daisy. Perfect names. And perfect pets for Nan. They can help in the garden and look after the dogs when I take them to visit, and whenever she snores she can say it's the cats."

"Does she snore?" asked Charlie.

"She says not," replied Lulu.

"And is she still mad that you and Mellie opened that bag?"

"Not at all," said Lulu. "She's very happy! She said thank you! That's what she said. 'Thank you, thank you, thank you!' And she said, over and over, 'I knew there was more than one cat in that bag.'"

Turn the page for a
sneak peek at the next

Lulu

adventure!

When Lulu discovers her next-door neighbor isn't very interested in his rabbit, she decides he is missing out on the best parts of having a pet. Can Lulu find a way to show him rabbits are fun?

Chapter One

More than Lulu and Mellie Could Bear

All the houses on Lulu's street were very small. "Like Lego houses," said Lulu.

They really did look like toy houses. They had brightly colored doors and flowerpots of flowers and gardens in the back like a row of patchwork squares.

Lulu's house had a green door and a dog's water bowl by the doorstep. Her cousin Mellie, who lived farther down the street, had a yellow door, which she had been allowed to paint herself for a birthday present.

Some people said the street was friendly. Other people said it was nosy. Lulu and Mellie were both friendly and nosy.

At the beginning of summer vacation, when a new family moved into the house next door to Lulu's, they couldn't help watching.

The new family was a father and a mother and a boy. They arrived with a big white van. Lulu and Mellie sat on Lulu's doorstep and watched it being unloaded until Lulu's mother made them come inside.

"It's nice to say hello and be friendly," she told them. "But sitting there staring is too much!"

"We offered to carry things," said Lulu, "but they said no thank you."

"Politely," said Mellie. "They are very polite. And the boy's got an Xbox. We saw it. He carried it in and he didn't come out again."

"He's setting it up," said Lulu. "Let's go and help!"

But Lulu's mother said very firmly that they could not do this either, so they went up to Lulu's room and hung out her window.

That was when they saw that something had appeared in the garden next door.

"A rabbit hutch!" said Lulu, and she hunted out her pirate telescope so she could look at the hutch more closely. "A rabbit hutch with a rabbit in it!" she told Mellie triumphantly.

"Why would he have a rabbit hutch without a rabbit in it?" asked Mellie.

"He might have gotten the hutch and be saving up for the rabbit," said Lulu. "I had my hamster cage for ages before I managed to save up for my hamster."

"How old do you think he is?" asked Mellie.

"Older than us," said Lulu. "Eight?"

"Eight?" exclaimed Mellie. "He's not! He was tiny! Six! Six, polite, interested in animals. What else?"

"He'll come out to see his rabbit soon," said Lulu. "Then we'll find out more."

However, the boy did not come out soon. Lulu and Mellie waited a long, long time before he appeared.

"At last!" said Mellie, yawning. She waved, but the boy didn't wave back.

"Shy!" said Mellie.

The boy walked down the garden carrying a bag. He went to the rabbit hutch. He opened the rabbit hutch door. He lifted out a china bowl and filled it with rabbit food out of the bag. He put the bowl back into the hutch and closed the door. Then he hurried back toward the house.

"There's lovely dandelions in his garden," said Lulu. "I wonder if he's noticed." She called, "Dandelions!" and pointed, but the boy did not look up. He went inside and he did not appear again. Lulu did not have a chance to talk to him until the next day.

"Hello!" she called.

"I'm busy," said the boy and turned his back.

It was difficult to talk to an unfriendly back, but by trying very hard Lulu managed. And she discovered that everything she and Mellie had guessed the day before was wrong. He wasn't six or eight; he was seven like them. He wasn't shy, and he wasn't at all interested in animals. Lulu found that out by saying, "We saw your rabbit yesterday!"

"Oh," said the boy (his name was Arthur) and shrugged.

"Was he all right, moving to a new house? Not muddled up or anything?"

Arthur turned around then and stared at Lulu as if she were crazy.

"I suppose he'll soon get used to
it, anyway," said Lulu. "And he'll like
exploring a new garden. There's good
dandelions in your garden. There's none
left in mine."

"I don't know what you're talking
about," said Arthur.

"Dandelions," said Lulu patiently.

"Because I've got two guinea pigs, and they like them just as much as the rabbits. I've got five rabbits. Four who live together because they're friends, and an only rabbit called Thumper who..."

"You have five rabbits?" demanded Arthur.

Lulu nodded proudly.

"Why would anyone want five boring rabbits?"

"They're not boring!"

"I've got one. That's enough. Five! What do you do with five rabbits?"

"Lots of things!"

"Do you know what my one does?"

"What?"

"Nothing!"

"Why did you get him, then?"

"I didn't. My granddad did for my birthday. I told him exactly the game

I wanted for my XBox and he went and got me a boring rabbit! How fair is that?"

"Why did he?" asked Lulu.

"He says XBoxes are garbage, that's why."

"That's 'cause he's old," said Lulu wisely.

"He's not that old," said Arthur. "He still plays football! Anyway, he gave me that rabbit. George. He called it George…"

"Him, not it!" interrupted Lulu.

"It makes no difference!"

"It does! And why don't you give poor George to someone who does want him?"

"Mom won't let me," said Arthur at once. "She says Granddad would be upset. And you don't need to call him poor George! I look after him. I feed him and I check his water and I clean him out every single week."

That was true. Lulu knew it was true

because she and Mellie checked. They could see George's hutch quite clearly from Lulu's bedroom window. With Lulu's telescope they could see George sitting inside.

Day after day.

Week after week.

Twice a day, at breakfast time and dinnertime, Arthur visited George with food and water. Once a week on Saturday mornings, he put him on the ground, scooped all the sawdust out of the hutch into a black trash bag, and put in fresh sawdust. It didn't take long to do this. The whole job was over in just a few minutes.

During those few minutes George became a different rabbit.

A non-sitting rabbit.
He would begin
with hops.
    Then a stretch.
            Then he would begin
                to run. He ran
                faster and faster
                in a racing circle
all around the little garden.
Sometimes as he ran, he leapt, high
into the air. He ran until he had to
stop, panting so hard his sides went in
and out.

Then Arthur would pick him up and
put him back inside his hutch.

To sit there for another week.

It was more than Lulu and Mellie
could bear.

Look for more

Lulu

adventures!

Lulu and the Duck in the Park
978-0-8075-4808-8
$13.99

When Lulu finds a duck egg that has rolled out of its nest, she takes it to class to keep it safe. Lulu isn't allowed to bring pets to school. But she's not really breaking the rules. It's just an egg, after all. Surely nothing bad will happen…

Lulu and the Dog from the Sea
978-0-8075-4820-2
$13.99

When Lulu goes on vacation, she finds a dog living on the beach. Everyone in the town thinks the dog is trouble. But Lulu is sure he just needs a friend. And that he's been waiting for someone just like her...

About the Author

Hilary McKay is the eldest of four girls and grew up in a household of readers. After studying zoology and botany in college, Hilary went on to work as a biochemist. She became a full-time mother and writer after the birth of her two children. Hilary says one of the best things about being a writer is receiving letters from children. Hilary now lives in a small village in England with her family. When not writing, she loves walking, reading, and having friends over to visit.